T0381325

On The Other Side Of The Blackboard

Patricia Lukoschek

Illustrated By: Angel Dela Peña Jr.

ISBN: Softcover 978-1-4836-5608-3
Ebook 978-1-4836-5609-0

Rev. date: 07/12/2013

To order additional copies of this book, contact:
Xlibris Corporation
1-888-795-4274
www.Xlibris.com
Orders@Xlibris.com

Dedication

There are so many amazing people that I would like to thank for supporting me during this period of adjustment. These include my wonderful family and dear friends and three very important administrators: Gonzalo Moraga, Paulina Jacobs and Dr. Manuel Fuentes. A special word of gratitude should be mentioned to every janitor that opened the gate early in the morning and every teacher and secretary that gave me the key and the opportunity to be a part of their school family. And of course a gesture of love to every child that gave me a sticker in the hopes that I would return to their school.

Special Mention

I would like to also mention both of my grandmothers, Elli Lukoschek and Nieves Garcia. They were truly the foundations of my family and never stopped believing in me. Unfortunately, they passed away before I became fully credentialed. I hope and pray that they are both in heaven smiling down, knowing that their dream did come true.

Deciding to become an author was not my first choice as a profession. I was and always will be a teacher. With eighteen years as a full-time elementary school teacher behind me, I suddenly found myself without a teaching position. But I adored working with children and decided to continue working in education as a substitute teacher.

The fateful day when my principal gave me the dreadful news that I had lost my job will forever be etched in my mind. I was devastated and my world turned upside down. I had also lost my contract, insurance and benefits. They say that out of every storm comes a rainbow. My rainbow carne and showed me that in the classroom is where I needed to be. To this day, I treasure that decision. For out of it carne numerous golden opportunities and experiences that no other position would have ever brought me.

After ten years of substituting in numerous school districts, I acquired a new perspective on teaching. Gone were the days of a permanent classroom, consistent colleagues (more or less) and my own nest of thirty children. Now I was officially a substitute teacher. As a result of this experience, I put together some thoughts and ideas that I felt would be helpful to all teachers, substitutes and seasoned professionals alike. As with everything else in life, there have been highs and lows. Some of these experiences are included in these pages.

When a teacher gets sick, he/she calls a substitute. What does a substitute do when they get sick? They call a substitute too.

If you can find the school, a parking spot, the office, the teacher, the teacher's lounge/restroom, and the lesson plans all before 8:00a.m.- you are going to have a great day.

Invest in a good city map. Just because you have worked in the same district for years, does not mean that you know where every school is located.

Always have your lunch and clothes ready the night before. Sometimes you will have less than an hour to get to the school site.

You don't have to worry about setting your alarm clock anymore. The district sub-line wakes you up sometimes earlier than you would like.

Be sure to park outside the school, especially if you are subbing half day. Finding someone to open the gate during the school day may turn into a full day of work.

SCHOOL CROSSING
NO BLOWING OF HORNS

Be sure to read the street signs. Every school site has different days for street cleaning. Parking tickets come with the territory.

Always know where the nearest coffee houses and gas stations are just in case you need to "fuel up" before getting to your assigned school.

Find out where the bathrooms and lunchrooms are before the bell rings, otherwise you may take up all your recess time looking for them.

Be proficient in how to use the various microwaves. It is a fact that not all district schools have the same microwaves.

Expect your colleagues to address you differently. From "Who are you today?" to your professional name.

Friendships with the secretary, janitor, and principal are very important, especially in that order.

Communicate your expectations from day one, especially if you are working a long-term position. Students have a keen sense of who they can work with and who they cannot. Show them that you are in control.

Classroom rules may vary within the same grade-level. Always know what the rules are before the children come into the classroom. Knowledge is power.

LIBBY
ALYSSA
EDUARDO
LIBBY
DON
DON
Seat Plan

Preparation is the Key: Diligence, Fairness, Positive Attitude, Punctuality, Organization and a Smile.

Nametags and seating charts are a must. Respect is not gained by calling someone, "Hey you"!

Always leave the teacher a note on the students' behavior—even if there were no problems. Being absent is difficult enough. It's always nice to come back to your class and have some feedback on how the children behaved.

You automatically become a handwriting analyst. Your sanity depends on understanding the lesson plans left by the teacher.

Never accept a Physical Education class on a rainy day, unless you have a huge bag of tricks.

You soon become a chameleon—in order to adapt to your surroundings.

What grade are you teaching? What if there are no lesson plans? You make it happen anyway.

Schedule
Planner

Carry a monthly planner with you at all times. You'll never know when a teacher may need you to substitute. You do not want to promise the same day to two different teachers. Most of all, you don't want to pass up any opportunities for a job.

Always carry a sub-emergency plan kit, including age-appropriate activities, name tags, and educational/fun activities. Illnesses and family issues are not usually planned.

Don't ever for a moment feel that just because it is not your classroom, that you are not in some way touching those children, making their lives better because of your influence.

Welcome
Back to School!

There is nothing better than coming back to a prior school site where all the children run to you in hopes that you will be their substitute again.

What a great feeling it is when the children request you to return to a specific school site.

Students that were transferred years ago from the school you taught, start popping up and making you feel great that they recognized you. You realize you made a difference in their lives when they show you how happy they are to see you again.

Thank you!
Thank you!
we
u

You can fall in love with the children that you have only met once, as much as if they were your own.

At the end of the day, if you have a few stickers on your shirt and a few "thank you" notes in your pocket, you know you've made a difference.

GRADUATION

It may seem that a substitute teacher's job is only to maintain a classroom while the teacher is out, however, the rewards are endless.

What a wonderful blessing it is to make new friends that I never would have otherwise had the opportunity of meeting.

At graduation time, instead of saying good-bye to thirty children, you are actually visiting several schools and saying good-bye to many more students whose life you touched.

LETTERS

Dear Ms L,

You have been a big part of everything we have done here in 5th grade. When we think of you smiles are brought to us. We created great memories with you here at school and at camp. You weren't just a substitute to us. You were a regular joyful, fun, loveable teacher. As we look back at all our memories you will pop up. Thank you for being there for all of us. We will miss you.

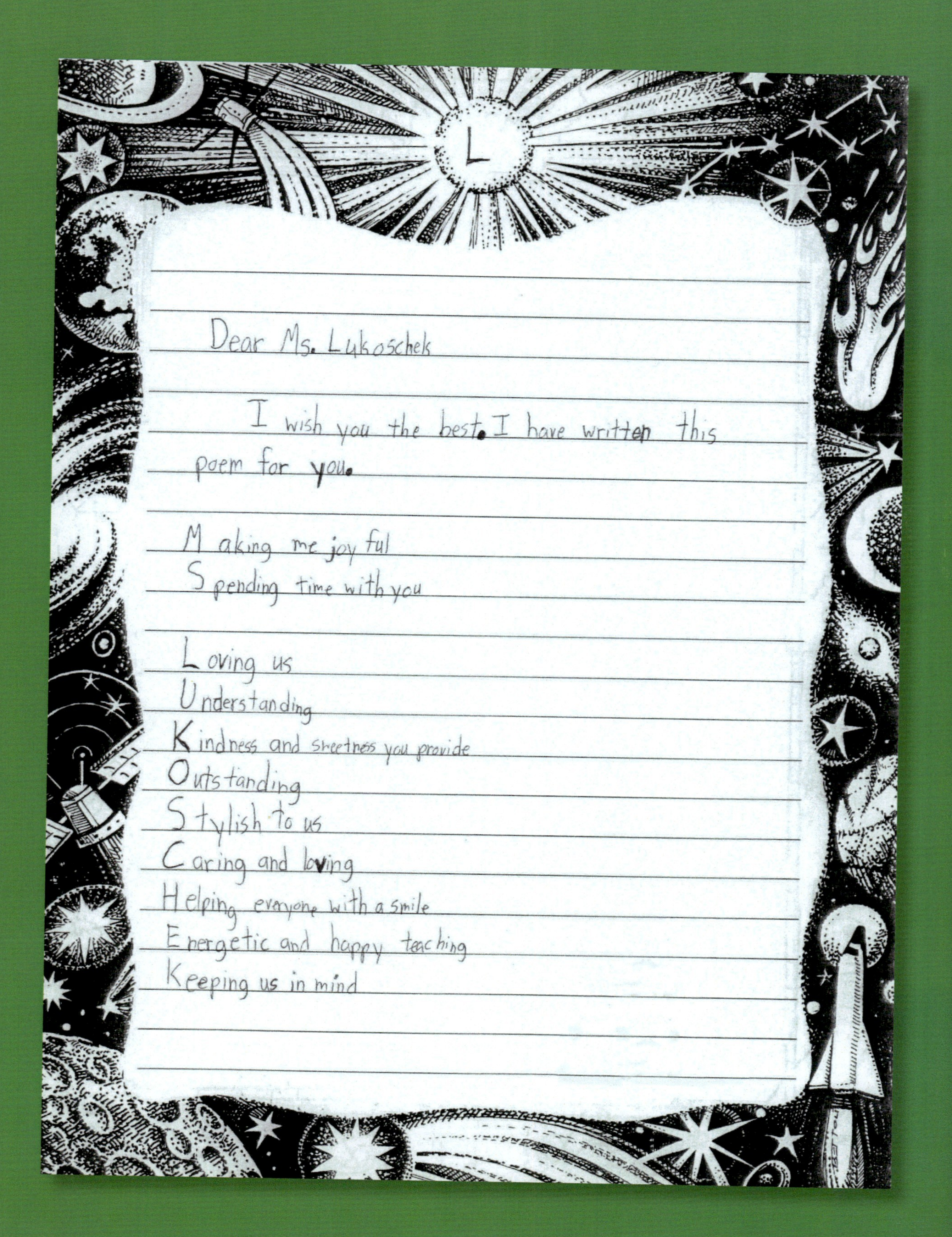
Dear Ms. Lukoschek

I wish you the best. I have written this poem for you.

Making me joyful
Spending time with you

Loving us
Understanding
Kindness and sweetness you provide
Outstanding
Stylish to us
Caring and loving
Helping everyone with a smile
Energetic and happy teaching
Keeping us in mind

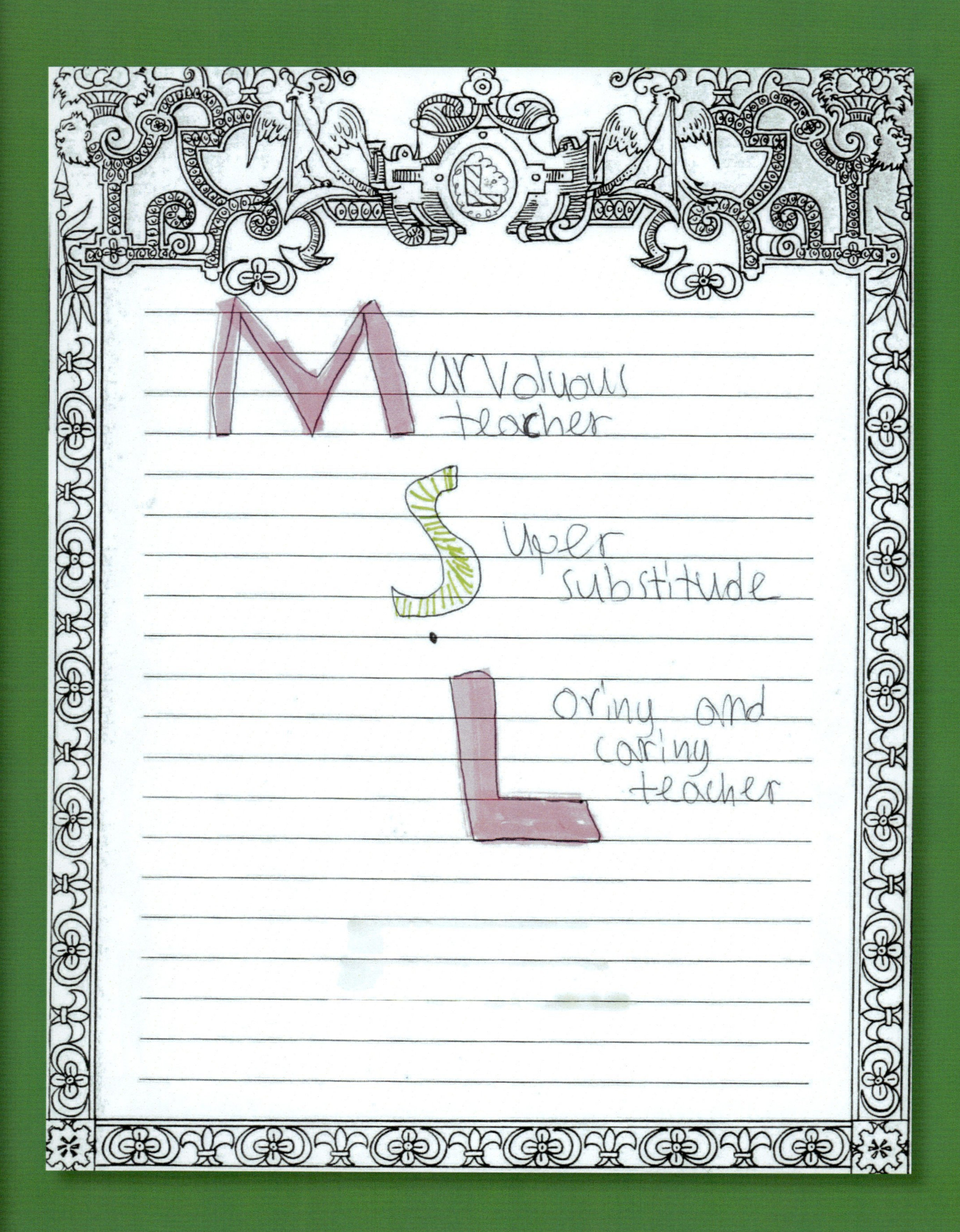
M
arvolous
teacher
S
uper
substitude
L
oving and
caring
teacher

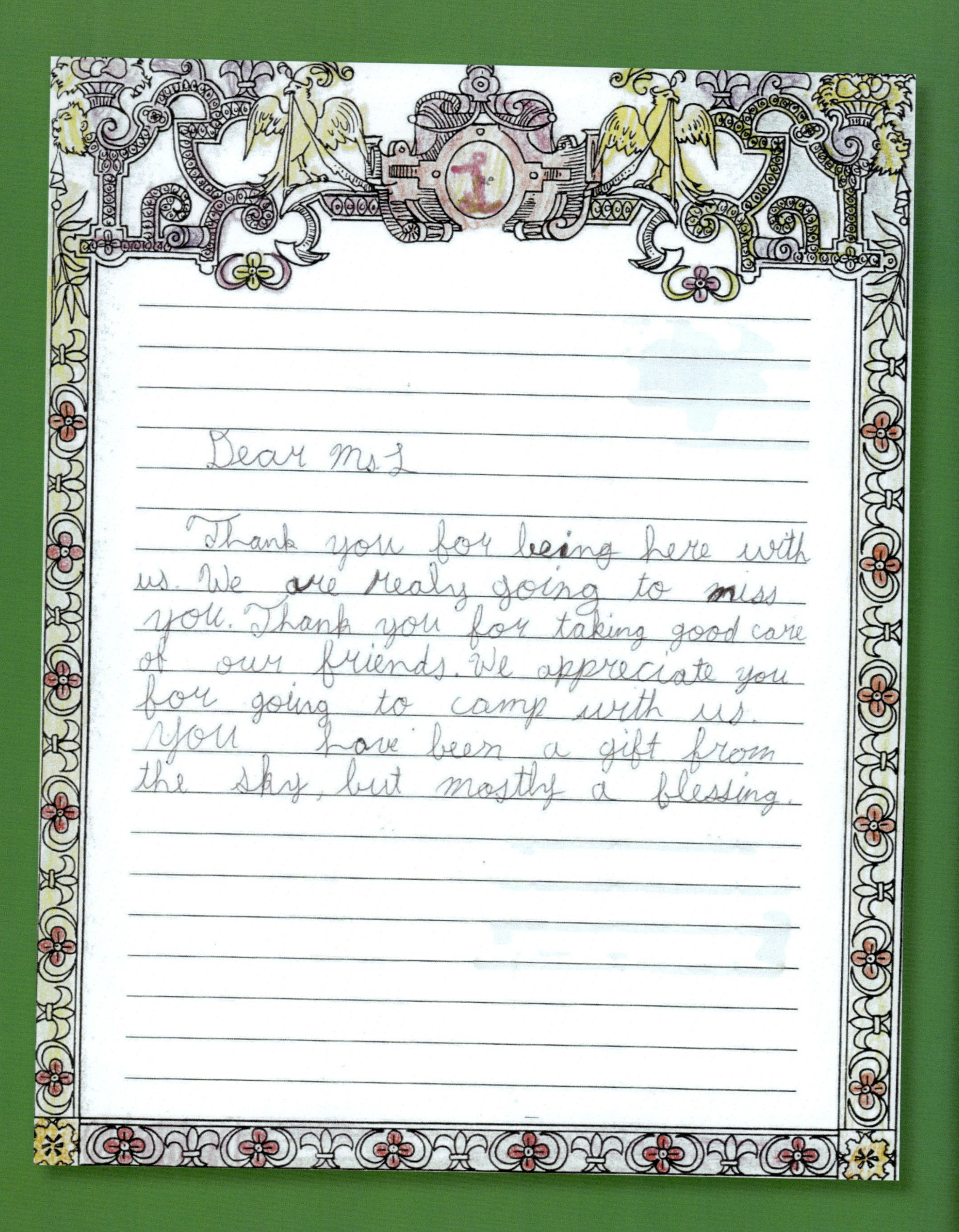

Dear Ms L

Thank you for being here with us. We are realy going to miss you. Thank you for taking good care of our friends. We appreciate you for going to camp with us. You have been a gift from the sky, but mostly a blessing.

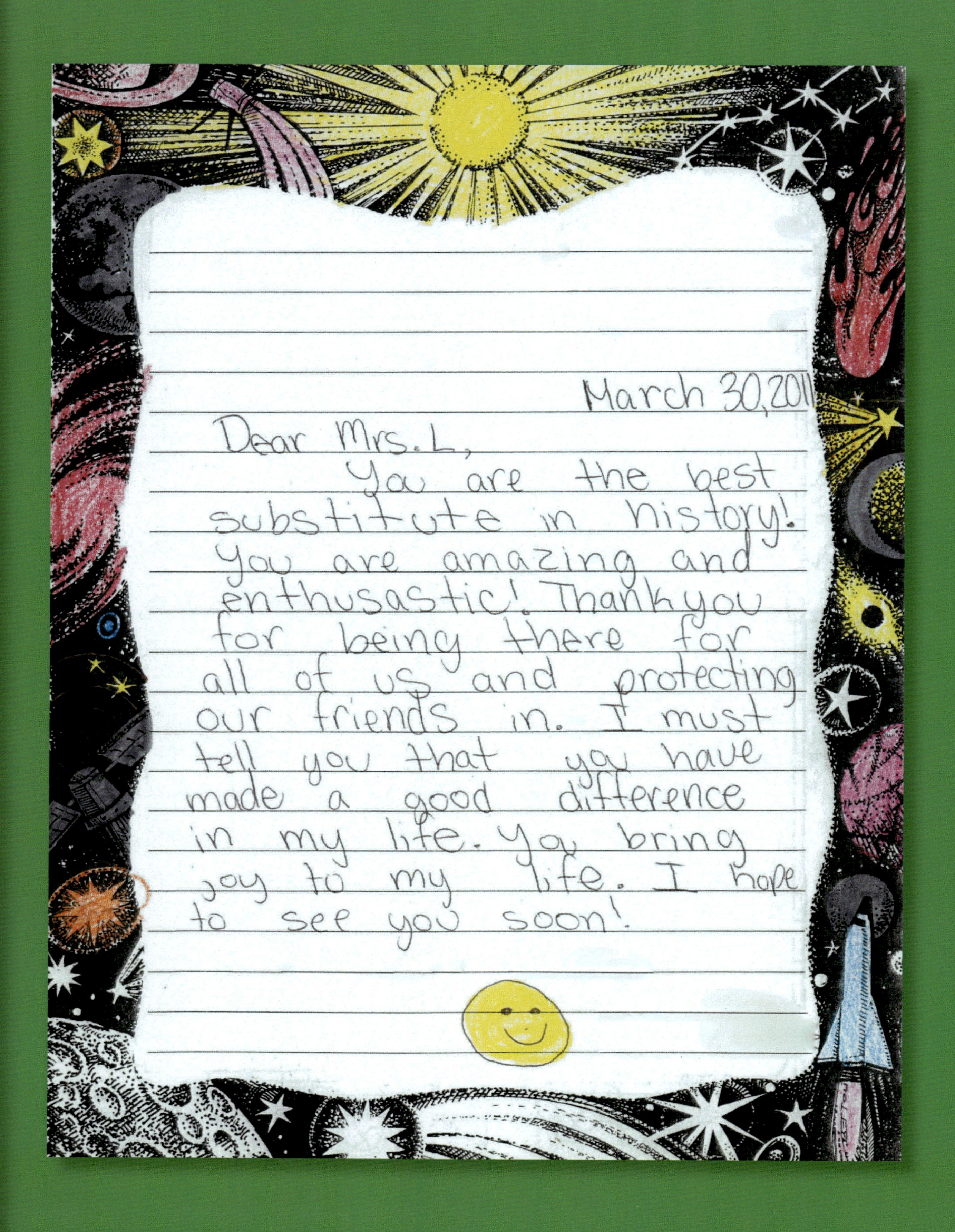
March 30, 2011

Dear Mrs. L,

You are the best substitute in history! You are amazing and enthusastic! Thank you for being there for all of us and protecting our friends in. I must tell you that you have made a good difference in my life. You bring joy to my life. I hope to see you soon!

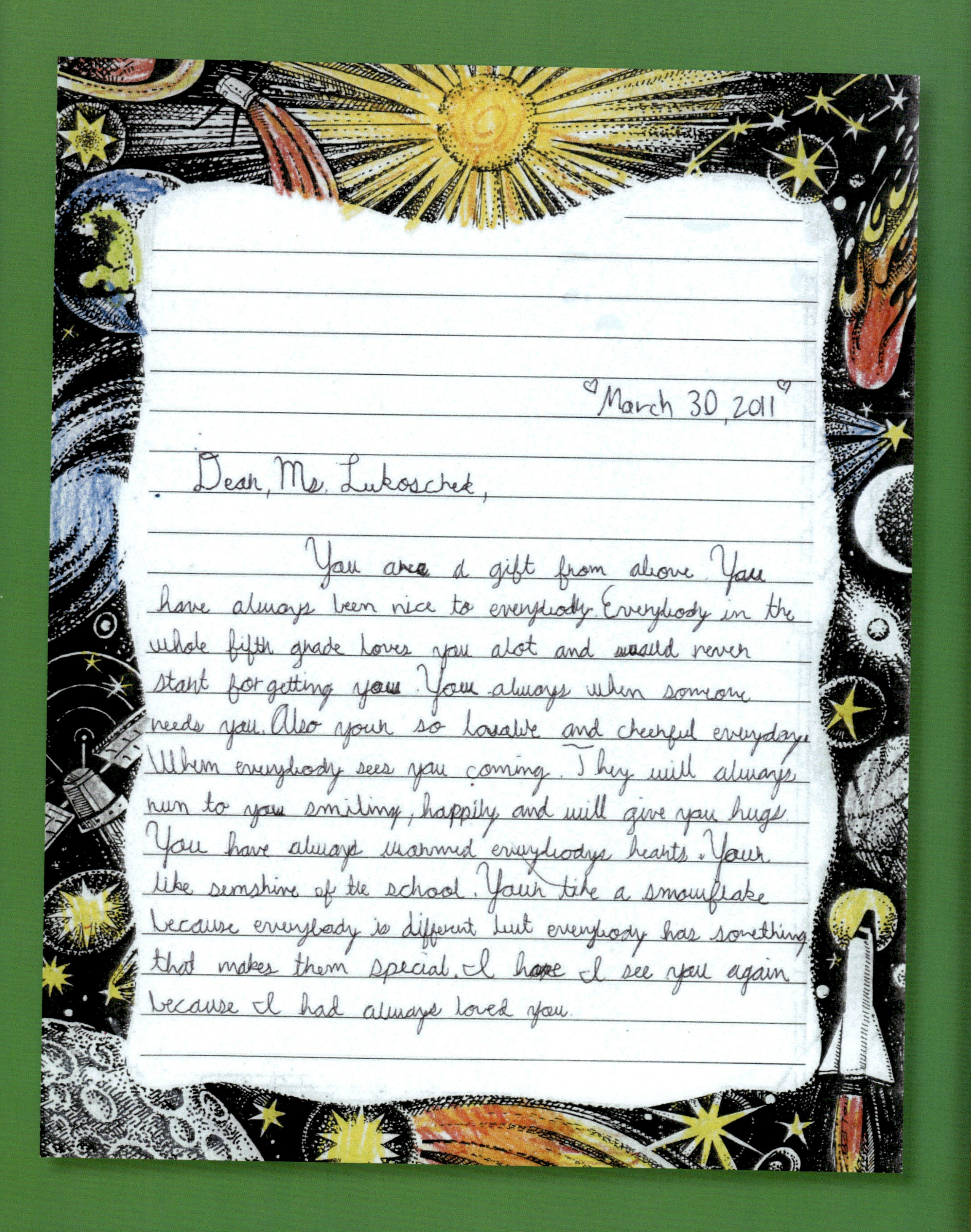

March 30, 2011

Dear, Ms. Lukoschek,

You are a gift from above. You have always been nice to everybody. Everybody in the whole fifth grade loves you alot and would never start forgetting you. You always when someone needs you. Also your so lovable and cheerful everyday. When everybody sees you coming. They will always run to you smiling, happily and will give you hugs. You have always warmed everybodys hearts. Your like semshine of the school. Your like a snowflake because everybody is different but everybody has something that makes them special. I hope I see you again because I had always loved you.

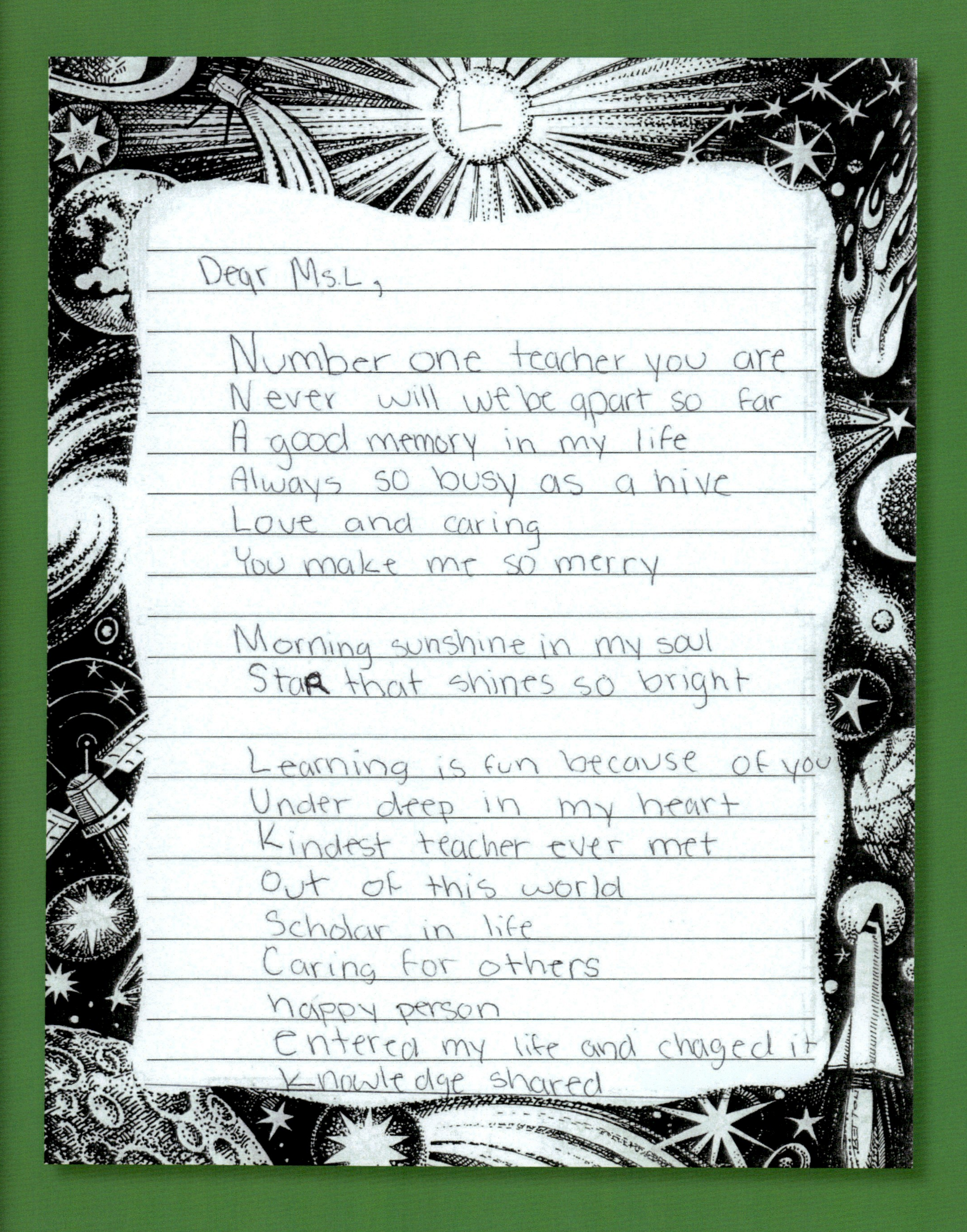

Dear Ms.L,

Number one teacher you are
Never will we be apart so far
A good memory in my life
Always so busy as a hive
Love and caring
You make me so merry

Morning sunshine in my soul
StaR that shines so bright

Learning is fun because of you
Under deep in my heart
Kindest teacher ever met
Out of this world
Scholar in life
Caring for others
happy person
Entered my life and chaged it
Knowledge shared

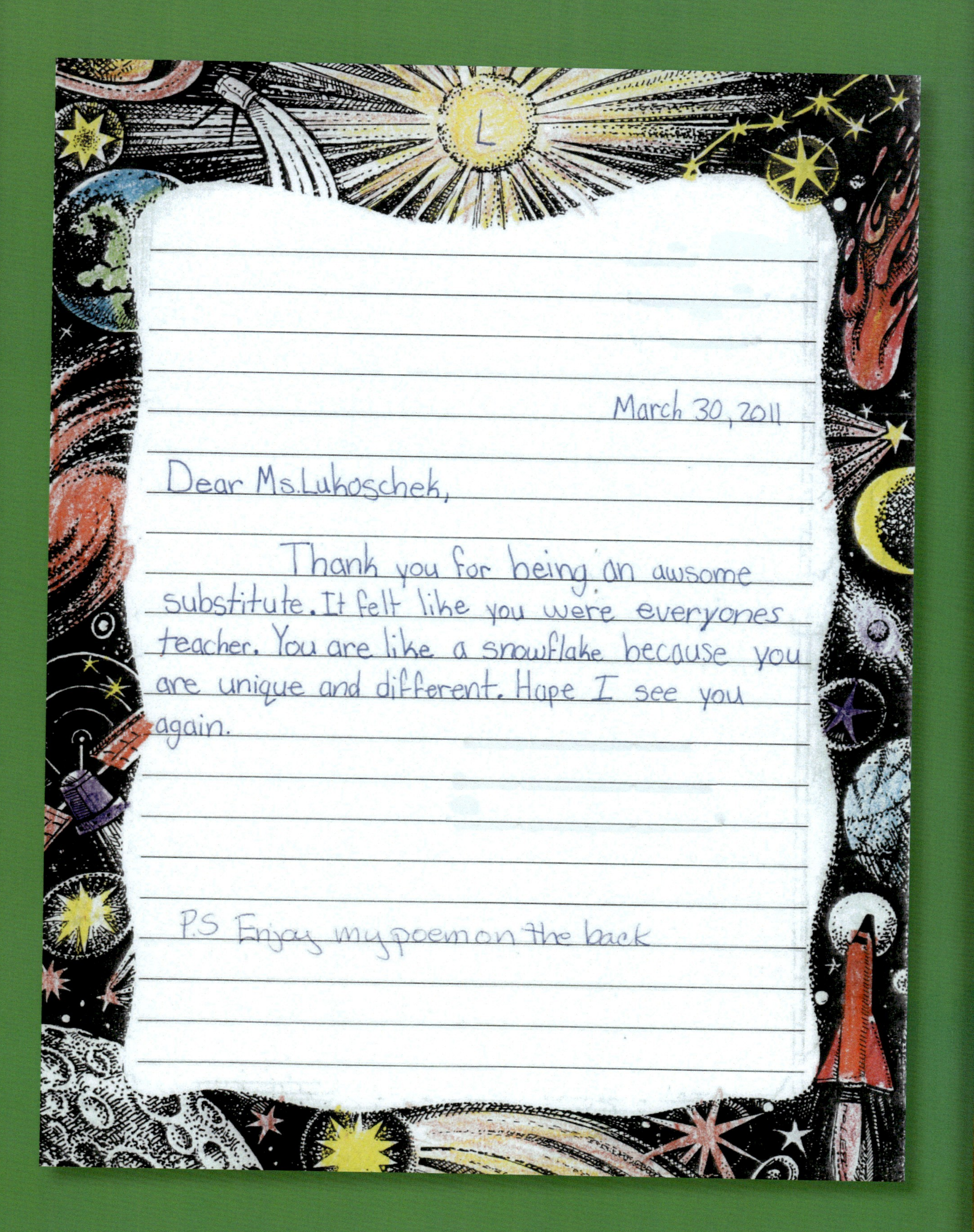

L

March 30, 2011

Dear Ms.Lukoschek,

Thank you for being an awsome substitute. It felt like you were everyones teacher. You are like a snowflake because you are unique and different. Hope I see you again.

P.S Enjoy my poem on the back

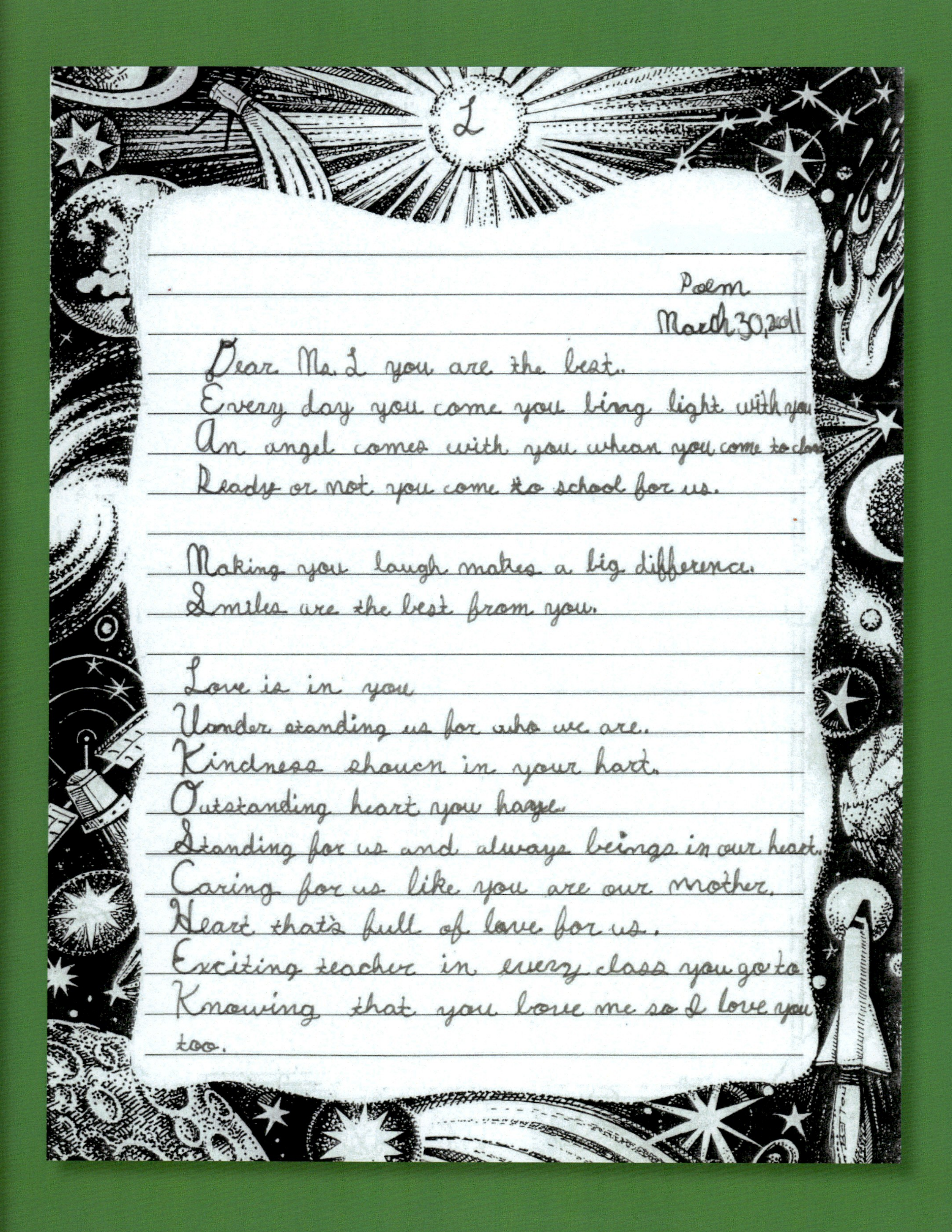

L

Poem
March 30, 2011

Dear Ms. L you are the best.
Every day you come you bing light with you
An angel comes with you when you come to class
Ready or not you come to school for us.

Making you laugh makes a big difference.
Smiles are the best from you.

Love is in you
Under standing us for who we are.
Kindness shoucn in your hart.
Outstanding heart you have.
Standing for us and always beings in our heart.
Caring for us like you are our mother.
Heart that's full of love for us.
Exciting teacher in every class you go to.
Knowing that you love me so I love you
too.

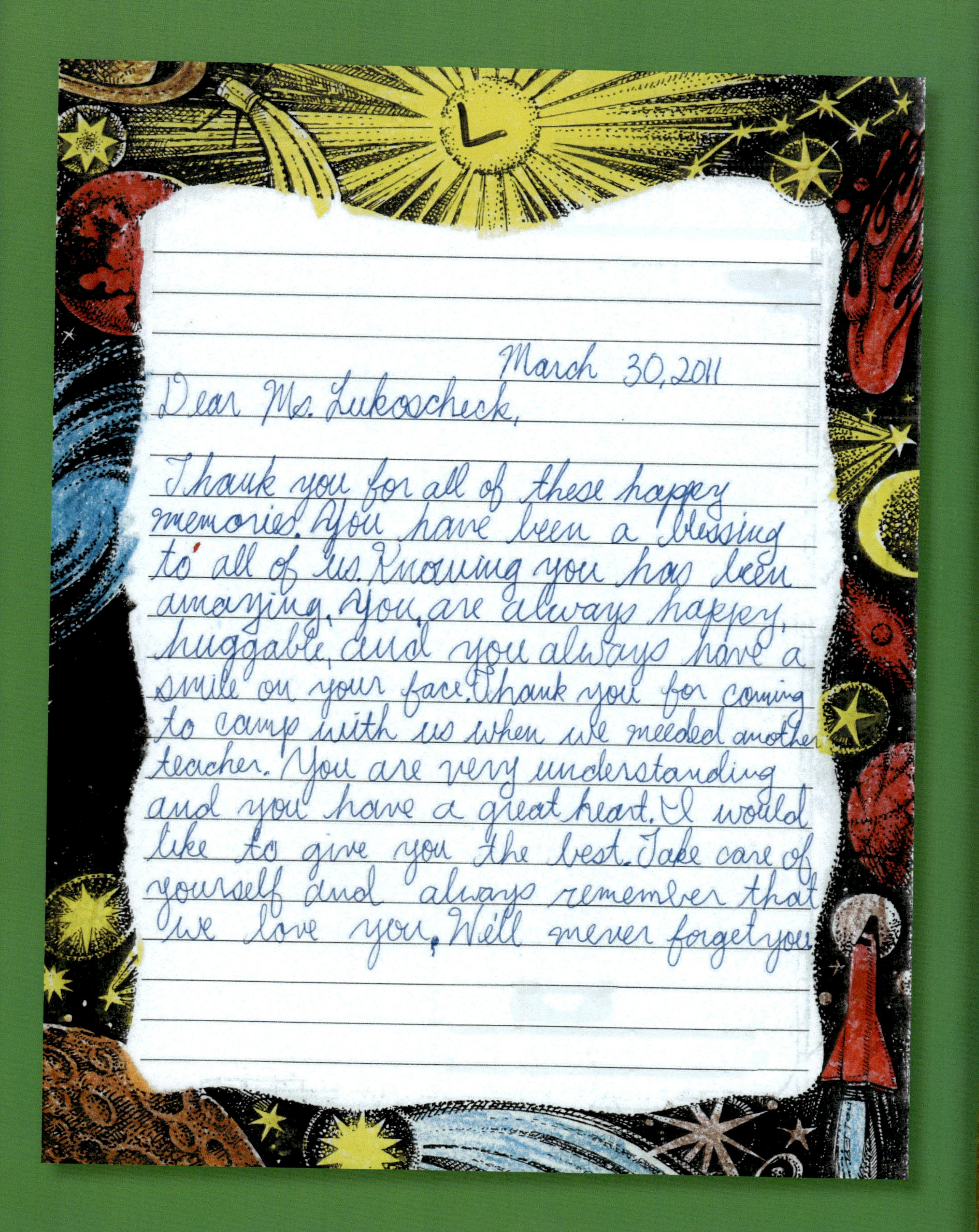
March 30, 2011
Dear Ms. Lukoscheck,

Thank you for all of these happy memories. You have been a blessing to all of us. Knowing you has been amazing. You are always happy, huggable, and you always have a smile on your face. Thank you for coming to camp with us when we needed another teacher. You are very understanding and you have a great heart. I would like to give you the best. Take care of yourself and always remember that we love you. We'll never forget you.

March 30, 2011

Dear Mr. L

I'm glad you have been here to substitute. We will miss you forever and remember the beautiful memories we have had. The days and minutes you have spent together with us are precious and unbreakable. Without you at camp we wouldnt have had that great experience. You filled us with hope and love, care and laughter, and faith in life. May God bless you and keep you safe everyday, everyminute, every second, all the time. Keep us all in your heart and I will always keep you in my heart too

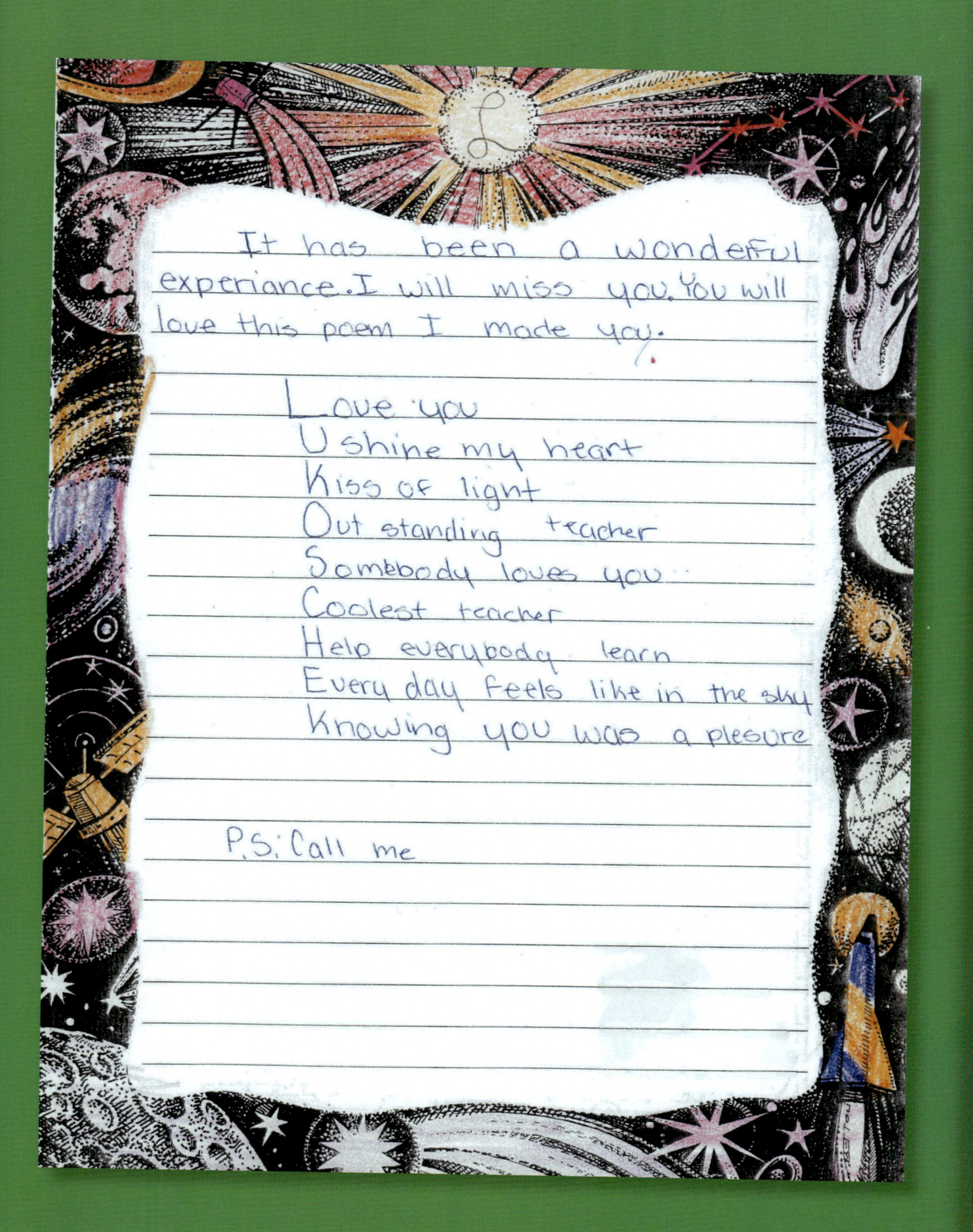

It has been a wonderful experiance. I will miss you. You will love this poem I made you.

Love you
U shine my heart
Kiss of light
Out standing teacher
Somebody loves you
Coolest teacher
Help everybody learn
Every day feels like in the sky
Knowing you was a plesure

P.S. Call me

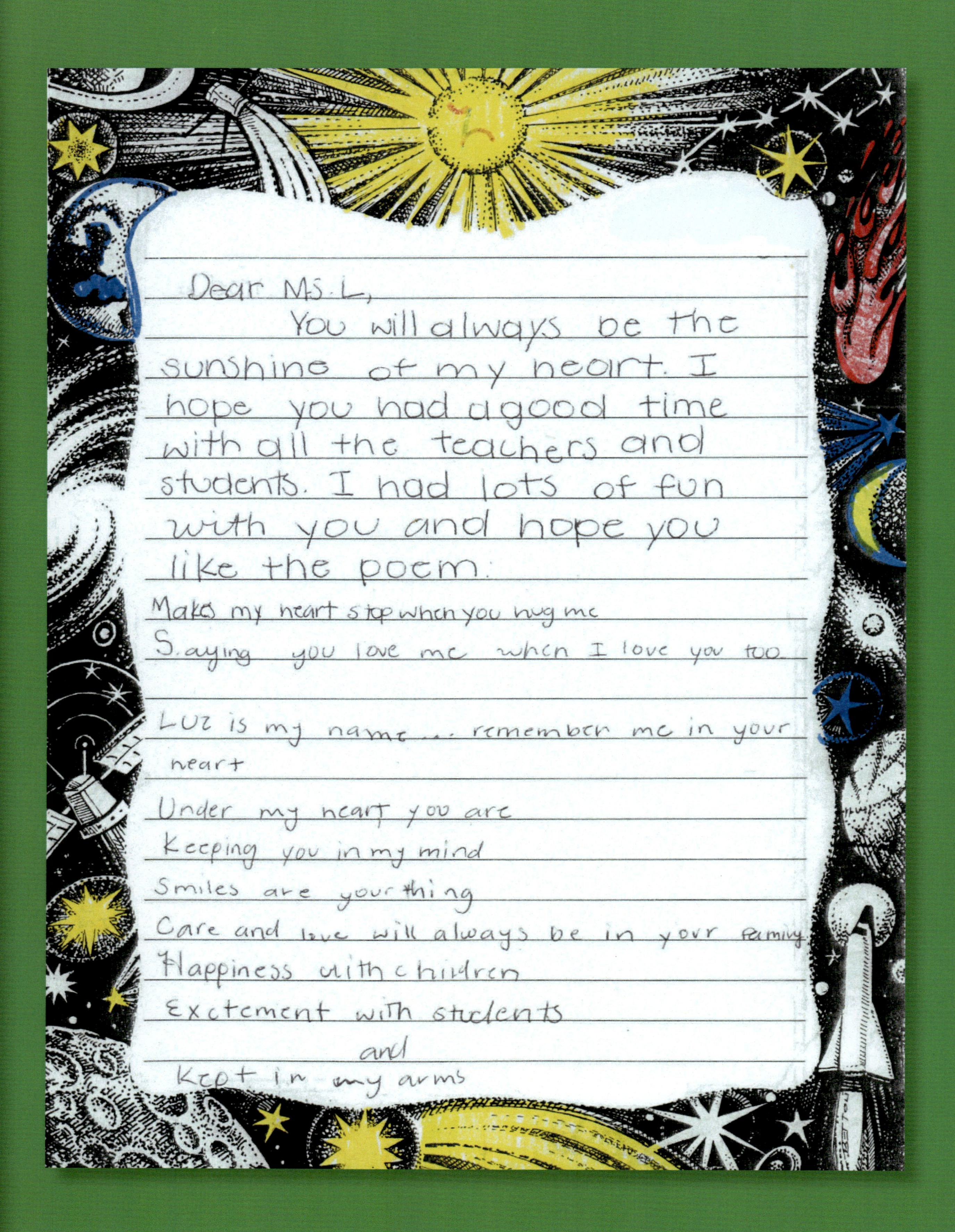

Dear Ms. L,

You will always be the sunshine of my heart. I hope you had a good time with all the teachers and students. I had lots of fun with you and hope you like the poem:

Makes my heart stop when you hug me
S.aying you love me when I love you too

Luz is my name... remember me in your heart
Under my heart you are
Keeping you in my mind
Smiles are your thing
Care and love will always be in your family
Happiness with children
Excitement with students
and
Kept in my arms